Dracula!

The very name conjures up visions of evil, of strange-
ness, of mystery. Now you and Indiana Jones™ are off
on a dazzling adventure to look for the priceless goblet
buried with the remains of the legendary Prince.

Your quest is vitally important, for it is said that whoever
drinks from the goblet will possess eternal life. You
don't want such power to fall into the wrong hands.

You'll have many decisions to make on your journey.
You will choose your actions and decide your own fate
by following the directions at the bottom of each page.

Make the right choices and you'll be a hero.

Make the wrong moves and...anything can happen.

Good luck! And be careful....

INDIANA JONES

JONES ™

and the
CUP OF THE
VAMPIRE

by Andrew Helfer

Illustrated by DAVID B. MATTINGLY

BALLANTINE BOOKS • NEW YORK

Other Indiana Jones_{TM} books in
the Find Your Fate_{TM*} Series
Published by Ballantine Books:

INDIANA JONES_{TM} AND THE CURSE OF
HORROR ISLAND

INDIANA JONES_{TM} AND THE LOST TREASURE
OF SHEBA

INDIANA JONES_{TM} AND THE GIANTS OF THE
SILVER TOWER

INDIANA JONES_{TM} AND THE EYE OF THE
FATES

RLI: $\dfrac{\text{VL: 5 + up}}{\text{IL: 5 + up}}$

Copyright ©: 1984 Lucasfilm Ltd. (LFL)
TM: A trademark of Lucasfilm Ltd.
Used under authorization
"Find Your Fate" is a Trademark of Random House, Inc.

Library of Congress Catalog Card Number: 84-91043

ISBN 0-345-31905-2

Designed by Gene Siegel

Cover and interior art by David B. Mattingly

Manufactured in the United States of America

First edition: October 1984

INDIANA JONES
and the CUP OF THE VAMPIRE

Find Your Fate™ #5

"Dracula, with this stake I shall destroy you forever!"

Your heart skips a beat when Dr. Van Helsing drives a wooden stake into the heart of Dracula, King of the Undead. You shudder as the vampire shrieks in horror and his body begins to shrivel up. Soon all that is left in the coffin is a pile of dust. Then the theater lights go up. "Wow!" you say to the man next to you. "That was some movie!"

But Indiana Jones does not respond. He is looking at his pocket watch and rubbing his chin nervously. "Where could Mihail be?" Indy says. "He's never late."

You met Indy just a few weeks ago during your summer job at the National Museum, but you can see that he is worried about his friend Mihail Tepes, the famous European archeologist.

Suddenly the doors at the back of the theater swing open, and a tall thin man stumbles down the aisle toward you and Indy.

"Jones," the man whispers in a heavy Eastern European accent, "they're after me. You've got to stop them!"

"Mihail!" Indy cries, jumping to his feet. Just then the theater doors fly open again, and four burly men in black overcoats bolt into the theater. Shocked, you realize that they are running toward you!

....

Turn to page 2.

"Indy!" you whisper as the men rush down the aisle. "What'll we do?"

Indy is busy holding up his exhausted friend. "Looks like it's up to you, kid!" he says.

Suddenly you remember the box of sourballs in your pocket. You grab a handful of the round candies and toss them into the aisle. They work like a charm! As your attackers rush at you, they slip and slide on the sourballs and crash to the ground!

"Good work, kid," Indy grunts, slinging Mihail's arm around his shoulder. "Now let's get out of here—that candy won't hold them off for long!"

You follow Indy and Mihail as they stagger through a nearby exit door. In seconds you are on the streets of Washington, D.C.

Go on to page 3.

"That way," Mihail says, pointing to a small Romanian restaurant down the street. "We'll be safe in there."

In moments you are seated in the dimly lit restaurant. "Okay, Mihail," says Indy. "What's the story? Who were those thugs back there—and why'd you set up this meeting in the first place?"

"It is a long story," says Mihail. "It concerns my ancestors in Romania—and the Cup of Djemsheed."

"The cup!" Indy whispers. "Solid gold. Encrusted with jewels. Stolen from a mosque in Persia during the sixteenth century and lost ever since. I remember a legend about it, the one that says that—"

"—That when filled with human blood, it will give whoever drinks from it eternal life!" Mihail finishes. "I followed the trail of the cup to my homeland of Romania, Indy, only to make a shocking discovery—I am a Dracula!"

··
Turn to page 4.

"Indy, I don't know about this guy," you whisper. "Let's get out of here!"

"Hang on a second," Indy replies. "This sounds interesting."

"Thank you, Indy," Mihail says. "I did not wish to alarm you or your friend, but what I say is true. I am the last living member of the Draculas, the royal Romanian family. Perhaps you do not know this, but Dracula was a respected name until the sixteenth century. Then my ancestor Prince Vlad Dracula became known throughout the land as a bloodthirsty tyrant. After he died, peasants insisted that he had cheated the grave. They said he had become one of the undead—a vampire who walked the earth eternally, drinking the blood of those still living!"

"I don't believe this," Indy mutters, shaking his head.

"But it is true!" Mihail protests. "I suspect that my ancestor discovered the Cup of Djemsheed and has used it to stay alive through the centuries! Even now, I fear that he feeds on the blood of innocent Romanians, and I—"

Mihail suddenly falls silent and stares off into the distance. You turn to see that the four men from the movie theater have just entered the restaurant!

....

If you think it's time to confront the men, turn to page 24.

If you think you're better off trying to escape, turn to page 41.

4

Ignoring the fact that all three of you have been struck speechless by his remark, the old man places a bottle of brandy on the table. Then he brings three crystal snifters and a jewel-encrusted golden goblet to the table.

"I only use this one for extra-special occasions," he says, holding the golden chalice before you. The three of you can hardly believe your eyes—it is the Cup of Djemsheed!

....

Turn to page 54.

The Gypsy drops Indy to the ground with a thud. Then he storms off, only to return with the dueling weapons. Indy is pleasantly surprised to see that the Gypsy has brought a pair of bullwhips.

"No thanks," Indy says when the Gypsy offers him a choice of the two whips. "I have my own." Indy reaches into his jacket and pulls out his whip. In seconds he is cracking it expertly in the air.

You, Mihail, and the Gypsies gather on the sidelines as Indy and his challenger take their places. You are expecting a long, painful battle, but it is over in a flash. With a single flick of his whip, Indy snatches his opponent's weapon from his hand. Then he cracks his whip at the Gypsy's suspenders. The huge man's pants fall down, and as he sputters in rage, the crowd roars with laughter.

Defeated and humiliated, the Gypsy sulks off. "I shall get my revenge," you hear him vow angrily, "if it is the last thing I do."

Turn to page 22.

You are walking up the slippery steps when you hear angry voices coming from the top of the stairs.

"The Romanian Anti-Vampire League!" Mihail whispers urgently. "They are after us again! We must hide—but where?"

"In here!" Indy says, motioning toward an open doorway. As the three of you pile into the dark room Indy trips over something. You hear the sound of clanking metal as he tumbles to the cold stone floor.

"What th—?" Indy whispers. "Mihail, shed some light on this, will you? But be quiet about it—if those Romanians find us here we're finished!"

As the angry voices above grow louder, Mihail uses his lighter to illuminate the small room. In the sudden burst of light you see a bejeweled skeleton lying on the ground. In its hand is the Cup of Djemsheed!

Turn to page 30.

"All right, kid," Indy says. "I'm gonna try and land this baby! Wish me luck!" Indy pushes the steering column forward and the plane swoops down toward the ground, brushing over treetops before coming to a screeching halt in an open field.

"Wow!" you say as you step onto firm ground once again. "We sure were lucky to survive that!"

"Luck had nothing to do with it," Indy replies. "That was skill." Then he turns to Mihail. "Any idea where we are?"

"It seems that our luck is still holding out," Mihail replies, pointing to a large stone castle not far away. "Because that, my friends, is Castle Dracula!"

"Great! Let's go," says Indy. Then you see that the only way to the castle is through an ancient graveyard.

Mihail leads the way past the cemetery gates, and you and Indy follow. Suddenly Mihail stops—in front of a stone mausoleum with the name DRACULA carved on it. As you approach, you see that the door is open!

....

If you decide to take a look inside, turn to page 117.

If you decide to continue on to the castle, turn to page 18.

Following Indy's orders, you zigzag away from the gunfire, taking cover behind the huge boulders scattered across the mountainside.

Soon the sound of gunfire fades. But the blizzard grows worse! The snow begins to fall so thickly that you can hardly see your hand in front of your face.

"Indy!" you shout, wandering blindly. *"In-deee!"* As you stagger through the snow, screaming for help, you hear another voice.

"Indy?" you call.

"Indy?" the voice responds.

"Where are you?" you shout.

"Where are you?" the voice answers.

You run toward the voice, but as you feel the ground beneath your feet give way to thin air, you realize that it was only an echo, and you have just stepped off the side of a mountain in search of your own voice!

Your journey has come to an abrupt...

END

"Those hunters!" the old man mumbles as you follow him through the woods. "They're always setting traps for the poor wolves. They think the wolves are a menace—but I know better! They're my friends, you see. My furry little friends..."

As the old man continues to babble, you hear the howling of the wolves again. You are beginning to think that following the man to his cottage wasn't such a good idea after all.

"This guy's a wacko," Indy whispers in your ear. "But play it cool. I don't think I can find our way out of these woods alone. Besides, it sounds like there are hungry wolves all around us now!"

Soon you reach a cottage in a small clearing. The old man is just about to open the front door when a pack of wolves leaps out from the woods. Their sharp pointed teeth bared, they circle around you, Indy, Mihail, and the old man. Instinctively, you reach for the gun under your belt.

....

Do you shoot at the hungry wolves? Turn to page 15.

Or do you wait to see what happens next? Turn to page 51.

11

Amid a hail of bullets, you, Indy, and Mihail crawl back toward the tunnel you noticed earlier. As the three of you huddle inside, you realize that you are slowly sliding down the slick, wet tunnel walls. Indy searches desperately for something to hang on to, but the tunnel walls are bare. The three of you continue to slide faster and faster, until you are plummeting at frightening speed.

"It's not the falling that worries me," Indy wails. "It's the landing that's gonna hurt!"

Below, you can hear the sound of rushing water, and seconds later you reach the end of the tunnel—only to be catapulted into the raging river of an underground cavern!

"Where are we?" you sputter as the swift current carries the three of you downstream.

"Who cares where we are?" Indy answers, pointing to the violently swirling whirlpool ahead. "That's where we're going—unless we think fast!"

Turn to page 29.

You cannot tell how long you have been unconscious, but when you awaken you are still inside the dusty coffin. You push against the lid, but to no avail. "Indy!" you scream, stricken with panic. "Are you there?"

"As usual, I'm right on top of things!" Indy yells from above. "Looks like the Friends of Dracula have stacked our coffins one on top of the other. I think you're in the middle—and that puts Mihail on the bottom."

"Correct," Mihail calls from below.

"Any idea where we're going, Indy?" you ask.

"I'm not sure," Indy replies, "but in the last twelve hours it feels like we've ridden on a plane, a truck, and in the luggage car of a train. Unless I miss my guess, we should be in Romania by now."

Suddenly the train screeches to a halt. For a moment there is silence. Then you hear a man's voice: "Hurry and open that safe! We haven't got all day!"

If you shout, you know you can get the man's attention. But are you sure you want to? It sounds like he's robbing the train! Who knows what he might do to *you*?

....

If you try to attract his attention, turn to page 43.

If you remain silent, turn to page 59.

13

The Lupan elder selects a young villager to lead you down from the mountains, and soon you are on your way. After you've traveled for many hours, the snow beneath your feet gradually disappears and lush green grass covers the ground. As the sun sets, you see a team of horses standing near an abandoned campsite in the distance.

"Looks like we're back in civilization!" Indy says happily. He tips his hat to the young Lupan, who smiles in return before he trots back up the mountains toward his home.

"Nice guy, that werewolf, eh, kid?" Indy asks.

You are about to agree when you feel a pair of arms grab you from behind. Immobilized, you watch helplessly as a band of Gypsies leaps from the trees to attack and subdue Indy and Mihail.

"We see you talk to evil werewolf," the Gypsy leader grunts as he unsheaths a sharp dagger. "You must be evil too—too evil to live!"

Turn to page 80.

You fire at the biggest wolf and it falls instantly. For a moment there is only silence. Then the old man rushes to the dying wolf's side.

"Natasha!" he wails mournfully. "What have they done to you!" He falls over the wolf's body, sobbing uncontrollably. When the other wolves begin to whimper and whine, you realize that you have made a terrible mistake.

Suddenly the old man looks up, hatred on his tear-stained face. "You three did this," he sniffles angrily. "You're no better than the hunters. And for hurting my Natasha, you will pay!" He waves his arm, signaling the other wolves to attack.

As they leap at you, you know that you cannot shoot them all. Sooner or later you'll run out of bullets, and then it will be...

THE END

Indy straps the parachute onto his back. "I'll be holding the two of you," he explains, "so as soon as we're in freefall, you pull the ripcord. Got that, kid?"

Before you can answer, Indy opens the escape hatch, grabs you and Mihail by the waist, and leaps from the plane. As you plummet through the icy sky toward the snowy mountains below, you pull the ripcord. The parachute blossoms open, and the three of you float lazily toward the earth. In minutes you land on the soft snow of the Transylvanian Alps. Huge mountains loom up all around you, offering a natural protection from the harsh winds.

"Good choice, kid," Indy says. "Now if we just knew where we were...."

Turn to page 76.

You continue walking through the graveyard, but when you hear the baying of hungry wolves nearby, you quicken your pace. The three of you rush through the graveyard exit toward the castle when you hear a man groaning in pain. You follow his voice and find a thin, bearded old man lying on the ground.

"Please," he moans, "help me."

Then you see the metal jaws of a beartrap locked around his ankle.

"Hang on a minute," Indy says, gripping the steel clamp. He pulls with all his strength, and soon the old man is free.

"Thank you," gasps the old man. "If not for you, I could have died here. I live in a cottage nearby," he continues, staggering to his feet. "Please, let me offer you a hearty meal. It's the least I can do to repay you."

"Why not?" Indy says, and the three of you follow the old man back to his home.

Turn to page 11.

As Indy pries the cup from the skeleton's hand, you hear the sound of running footsteps. In seconds, a familiar group of Romanians bursts into the room. They are armed with huge wooden stakes, and the airplane stewardess is among them.

"Ha!" she shouts. "All vampires come here sooner or later. We wait for you, and now we destroy you! The Anti-Vampire League triumphs once again!" The stewardess lets loose a blood-curdling cry as she and her companions rush toward you, their stakes pointed directly at your chest!

You panic and try to defend yourself by reaching for the first available object. Your hand finds the stake planted in Dracula's coffin.

"No! Don't!" you hear Mihail scream in terror, but it is too late.

Turn to page 69.

A gloved hand appears and brushes the spider off your nose.

"*Ka-CHOO!*" you sneeze.

"Gesundheit," a strange voice says.

"Thank y—" you begin, but your words die out when you get a good look at the strange man standing before you. His skin is pale white, in sharp contrast to his flowing mane of black hair. Beneath his handlebar mustache you can see a pair of deep red lips. And when he smiles, you see that his teeth are sharp and white.

The stranger's long black cape seems to float around him as he turns to face Mihail. "They should not treat you like this," he says sadly. "You, the last living member of the Dracula family."

As the man speaks, Indy eyes him carefully. "Don't I know you from someplace?" he finally asks.

Turn to page 31.

20

As the vanquished Gypsy stalks off into the woods, the other Gypsies gather around Indy. There are tears of happiness in their eyes. "Our leader was a cruel and dishonorable man," one of them tells Indy. "But you have defeated him in battle—and that makes you our new leader! How may we serve you, Indiana Jones?"

"We'd...uh...like to get to Castle Dracula, to find the Cup of Djemsheed," Indy says, uncertain if he is asking too much of the superstitious Gypsies. But they agree to take you to the castle! You travel all night, and by dawn you can see the ancient ruins atop a craggy hill in the distance.

"Your destination is before you," one of the Gypsies says.

But as he speaks, the sky suddenly darkens. It's filled with thousands of angry crows! The Gypsies scream in terror as the black birds descend on them.

"The devil is upon us!" the Gypsies cry, scattering in panic.

The crows follow, shrieking, and soon, you, Indy, and Mihail are alone once again.

"Well, at least we found the castle!" says Indy. "C'mon, kid. We've got some climbing to do!"

Turn to page 35.

"YIIIEE!" you scream at the top of your lungs. You've never been so frightened in your life! As you scramble out from under the centuries-old skeletons, you hear Indy whisper urgently.

"Quiet, kid!" he says. "You're screaming loud enough to wake the dead—and just think how crowded this place would get if *they* started walking around!" Then Indy turns to Mihail. "What do you make of this?" he asks.

"It appears to be the Dracula *family* crypt," Mihail answers. "Vlad Dracula himself must be buried elsewhere. Come, let us go to the castle. Perhaps there we shall find the prince."

You leave the burial room and are walking back through the narrow tunnel when you hear squeaking noises behind you. From the corner of your eye you see something black scurry along the floor. Rats—thousands of them—are coming straight for you!

Turn to page 58.

"I'm going to talk to them," you whisper to Indy. "They won't try anything funny here."

"What do you guys want?" you ask boldly.

The largest of the men reaches into his coat and produces a revolver. He points it at you. "No prisoners," he whispers angrily.

You freeze. You hear the click of the gun's hammer being pulled back. Then—

Crack!

From behind you, Indy's bullwhip lashes over your shoulder, knocking the gun out of the man's hand. "Get it, kid!" Indy shouts, pointing to the revolver spinning on the floor.

You reach the gun just as one of the men tackles you. He wrests the gun from your hands and presses it to your head.

Turn to page 47.

The three of you travel on horseback for many hours, and night has already begun to fall when the remains of a huge ancient castle loom up in the distance. Only a single tower is still standing among the ruins.

"That is our destination," Mihail proclaims. "Castle Dracula."

As you stare in awe at the huge stone structure you think you see a strange form scaling the tower. You blink in disbelief—is the light playing tricks on you, or has a *man* just crawled up the tower and in through its only window? You tell Indy, but he laughs. "You're imagining things, kid," he says.

In frustration, you race ahead to the castle. It's surrounded by a moat, but when you look into the clear water, you see that it is no more than six inches deep. You are anxious to cross the shallow moat and get a closer look at the castle. What should you do?

....

If you decide to cross the moat right away, turn to page 50.

If you decide to wait for Indy and Mihail before doing anything, turn to page 65.

25

You and Indy turn to the man, who lies on the floor, gasping for breath. Indy shakes him.

"Okay, buddy," he says. "What's the story? Why are you after us? Tell me or I'll—"

The man ignores Indy. With his eyes fixed on Mihail, he swiftly raises his hand to reveal a strange ring—a ring in the shape of a coffin! Before you can stop him, the man flicks open a secret compartment on the lid of the ring and swallows the pill hidden inside.

"You shall never make me one of your undead!" he exclaims. Then, still staring at Mihail, he gasps and shudders. He is dead!

Turn to page 82.

Despite your kicking and screaming, the black-robed Romanians drag you down to a barred room in the lowest level of the castle. Iron chains dangle from the walls. Your captors slam you against the wall and lock shackles around your wrists. Soon Indy and Mihail join you.

As the three of you dangle helplessly from the walls, Indy groans. "We're going to need a miracle to get out of this one, kid," he says. "Looks like we've had it."

"I can't believe it," you moan. "By midnight we're going to be an ingredient in some vampire-lover's Bloody Mary!" You glance at your watch. "We've got less than four hours to live!"

"Uh, kid," Indy says. "You might not even have *that* long. Take a look at your foot."

You look down and see a huge furry tarantula crawling up your leg. If you try to shake it off, you know it might bite you. So you hang there motionless as it crawls over your chest and up your neck before settling on your nose.

The spider's fur tickles your nostrils, and suddenly you get the urge to sneeze. "Ahh...ahhh..." you gasp.

Turn to page 20.

27

As the current sweeps you through the cavern toward the whirlpool, you notice a door carved into one of the stone walls around you. You swim frantically against the current, trying to edge your way over to it.

"You'll never make it that way!" Indy shouts above the raging waters. "I've got a better idea!" He sets his sights on the metal handle of the door and manages to crack his bullwhip at it. The tip of the whip wraps itself around the handle. "Got it!" Indy cries. "Now swim over to me and I'll try to haul us out of here!"

Once you and Mihail struggle over to Indy, he uses his whip to pull you both to safety. Before long you are standing on a narrow ledge in front of the door.

Wet and tired, you lean against the door. When you do, it creaks open to reveal a moss-covered staircase that leads up into the castle.

Turn to page 7.

"Dracula..." Mihail utters in awe, just as the doors behind you burst open.

"Friends of the demon," the airline stewardess announces, "your infernal luck has just run out!" The other Romanians point their guns at you, waiting for the command to fire.

"Wait!" Mihail exclaims. "The evil one you really want is dead—there are his remains to prove it!"

The stewardess is skeptical at first, but when Mihail shows her the bejeweled crown she is convinced.

"The last of the Draculas speaks the truth," she declares. "The evil Vlad Dracula is dead—and the curse of the vampire is broken! Now come, my brothers," she continues. "We have one more thing to do."

You, Mihail, and Indy watch as the Romanians place the skeleton in a cloth sack, leaving the Cup of Djemsheed lying on the ground.

"Uh, excuse me, ma'am," Indy asks politely, "but aren't you going to take that cup, too?"

"Certainly not," the stewardess replies. "We wish only to burn the bones of Vlad Dracula."

"Then you, uh, wouldn't mind if *we* took it along?" Indy asks. "Sort of like a souvenir?"

"Take it," the stewardess replies. "Now come with us. We'll give you a lift to the airport."

Indy winks at you as you head out of the castle—with the legendary Cup of Djemsheed!

THE END

The stranger says nothing. Instead, he reaches into his pocket and removes a skeleton key. In seconds he unshackles the three of you and points to a nearby stairway.

"You must leave now," he says. "Before it is too late. The Friends of Dracula will be punished severely for what they planned to do to you. Go now— or join them in their fate."

"You don't have to tell us twice," Indy answers as he runs toward the stairs. He takes them two at a time, with you and Mihail following hot on his heels.

The main doors of the castle are at the other side of a large hall at the top of the stairs. As you run toward the doors, an old painting in a massive gold frame catches your eye. It is a portrait of the stranger who rescued you! And at the bottom of the frame is a brass plaque bearing the subject's name: PRINCE VLAD DRACULA!

Turn to page 97.

You, Indy, and Mihail follow the werewolf through a snowy mountain pass. On the other side, you see the village of the Lupan: five simple wooden cottages arranged in a circle. In the center a group of werewolves talk among themselves. But when they see you approaching, they fall silent.

"I'm not sure I like the looks of this," Indy mutters as the group of werewolves begins to walk toward you.

"You must forget your superstitious nature, Indy," Mihail says as he waves and smiles at the approaching werewolves. "The Lupan are not werewolves—they are merely victims of a

peculiar disease that causes hair to grow all over their faces and bodies. In every other respect they are normal. But their strange appearance made them feared and hated by the superstitious peasants. They fled the villages and settled here, seeking only peace."

As the werewolves come closer, they unsheath sharp swords from scabbards hidden under their clothes. They encircle the three of you, swords high in the air, ready to strike.

"Some peace," Indy groans.

··

Turn to page 84.

"We surrender!" you shout, raising your arms high in the air.

The three men point their guns at you, Indy, and Mihail as they make their way down the mountainside.

"So these are the Friends of Dracula," Indy mutters. "They don't look so tough to me!"

"The Friends of Dracula?" says one of the men with a grim chuckle. "Oh, no, Mr. Jones. You are mistaken. We are not the Friends of Dracula—we are just three humble mercenaries trying to earn a living. But we *are* working for the Friends of Dracula. They offered us a large reward to capture Mihail Tepes. Unfortunately he was with you, and he escaped." The mercenary looks at Indy coldly. "But you will not escape again." He jabs a gun at you. "Now come along," he says. "We go to the castle. It is just over that hill."

Turn to page 86.

For long hours you, Indy, and Mihail crawl over huge rocks and between narrow crevices, slowly making your way to the top of the hill. On the way up you pass a small dark cave. You are about to tell Indy about it when you hear gunshots.

"Get down, kid!" Indy shouts. "Stay close to the rocks—that'll make us a tougher target!"

"But who's shooting at us?" you ask.

"See for yourself!" Indy says, pointing up toward the top of the hill. "But be careful!"

You poke your head above the rocks and see the airline stewardess and two other Romanians. They stand by the castle doors with rifles in their hands. "What do we do now?" you shout to Indy in panic. "We're sitting ducks!"

"Not quite," Indy replies, gesturing toward a huge rock about ten feet above you. "If we can avoid those bullets and get up there, we should be safe." But when Indy sees the uncertainty on your face, he frowns. "You got any better ideas, kid?" he growls.

If you suggest running down the hill to the cave, turn to page 12.

If you decide to go along with Indy's suggestion, turn to page 90.

Indy drinks the wine. "Good stuff," he says. "Have a glass, Mihail. You too, kid."

Mihail gulps down his wine and you take a small sip from the glass the stewardess hands you. The wine tastes bitter, but you drink it just to be polite.

Then, as the stewardess watches, you begin to feel drowsy. "Something's wrong," you mutter to Indy. But he has already fallen into a deep sleep! Then you too black out.

You awaken to find yourself lying in a deep pit alongside the still forms of Indy and Mihail. The stewardess and a group of Romanian peasants in black overcoats are standing watch over you, shovels in their hands. There are broad smiles on their faces.

"Another victory for the Anti-Vampire League!" the stewardess proclaims triumphantly. "Cover them up!"

As piles of dirt cascade down, you realize this is...

THE END.

You say good-bye to Sasha, and soon you are chasing your kidnappers through the Borgo Pass.

"C'mon, kid!" Indy shouts, following them down a narrow trail. "We're gaining on 'em!"

But farther up the trail a huge boulder blocks the way. It's a dead end—and the kidnappers have disappeared!

"What happened?" Indy asks, scratching his head. "One minute we're right behind them. The next—*poof*! They're gone!"

An icy chill runs down your spine. Human beings don't just vanish into thin air—but *vampires* do! At that moment a rumbling sound fills the air and an enormous boulder bounces down the mountainside toward you. You manage to leap out of the way in time, and the boulder lands in the middle of the trail, blocking your way out. Before you can catch your breath, a voice shouts down from the mountaintop: "Surrender or die!" Looking up, you see three heads poking out from behind another huge rock—the kidnappers!

Should you pretend to surrender? You've got a hunch that the kidnappers will lead you closer to Prince Dracula and the Cup of Djemsheed.

But you might be getting into more trouble than you bargained for. Maybe you'd better try and escape—while you have the chance!

....

If you pretend to surrender, turn to page 34.
If you try to escape, turn to page 56.

"Don't look down!" Indy shouts as the three of you scale the tower wall. You feel like you've been climbing for hours. Then, in the moonlight, you can see your destination—the open tower window. You feel a rush of excitement as you realize that the end of your quest is at hand.

Indy crawls in through the window, and you and Mihail soon follow. You are taking a moment to catch your breath when you hear strange squeaking noises and the fluttering of leathery wings. You can't see anything in the darkness, but the sounds are making you nervous. You reach into your pocket and pull out a book of matches.

"Think I'll throw a little light on this situation," you whisper to Indy.

"Wait a second, kid!" Indy responds urgently.

If you wait before doing anything, turn to page 85.

If you strike a match, turn to page 112.

38

On horseback you follow Sasha and his bandits through the Borgo Pass and into a lush green valley. By nightfall you are standing outside the ruins of Castle Dracula. The main entranceway remains intact, but all but one of the castle's towers have collapsed, and huge bricks of moss-covered granite lie scattered all around you.

Sasha runs toward the front doors. "In here!" he shouts, and his men quickly obey. The bandits enter the castle, leaving you, Indy, and Mihail behind.

"Hey!" Indy shouts as the three of you rush to catch up. "*I'm* supposed to be giving the orders here! Who's in charge of this expedition?"

Just as you are about to enter the castle, you hear the sound of gunshots coming from inside. Carefully the three of you peer in through the door. What you see shocks you.

....
Turn to page 114.

"Through there, kid," Indy says, gesturing toward the restaurant kitchen. You, Indy, and Mihail leap from the table and bolt through the swinging doors. On the other side, two startled cooks turn from their simmering pots and pans to look at you.

"Hey!" one chef shouts. "You can't come in here!"

"We were just on our way out!" Indy answers, heading for a door marked "exit." "This way!" he calls to you. "They'll never expect us to use the back door!"

You race through the door and into an alley filled with loaded garbage cans. Suddenly three enormous shadows loom up on the wall before you. An instant later a blackjack lands solidly on the back of your neck and knocks you unconscious.

You awaken in the backseat of a limousine with Indy and Mihail. Both of them rub their heads gingerly. "Ooooh," Indy groans, "that plan didn't work too well, did it?"

There are three thugs seated in front of you. One is driving. The other two are watching you carefully, their guns pointed at your head.

"Make a move," one of them grunts, "and you're dead."

....
Turn to page 87.

41

Ancient tapestries line the cold stone corridors of the centuries-old Romanian National Library building, where Mihail introduces you to Radu Aldea, the head librarian. Radu takes you down to a huge steel vault in the library's lowest level.

"Behind these doors are some of Romania's greatest treasures," he explains. "Hand-drawn maps and papers from the Middle Ages. These documents are stored inside airtight, temperature-controlled glass cases to prevent them from disintegrating. Just this morning," he tells you, "someone broke into the vault. The collection of documents about Prince Vlad Dracula was disturbed. It is very curious that you wish to see them too!"

Radu tugs the door open. Behind a glass partition are stacks upon stacks of yellowing paper, all alphabetically arranged. Mihail rushes to the D section, removes a file of documents, and begins to leaf through it cautiously. "Indy!" he cries. "Look at this!"

Turn to page 70.

You kick at the lid of your coffin and pound your fists against its side. "Hey! Help us!" you scream. Seconds later your box is lifted up and placed carefully on the ground.

"This is quite amazing," the voice outside comments. "Few people in coffins can shout with such urgency!" Then strong hands tear away the coffin lid and a group of tough-looking, dark-haired men stare down at you before helping you up. As you dust yourself off, you hear muffled shouting coming from the other two closed coffins.

"Kid!" Indy calls from inside his coffin. "As long as you're out there, would you mind getting me out too?"

"Yes," Mihail adds from inside his coffin, "it *is* getting stuffy in here."

The men open Mihail's coffin and move on to Indy's. But the largest of the men motions the others away. "I know that voice!" he says. "This box I open myself!" Then he grips the coffin lid and tears it off.

As he looks inside, the man smiles. "Indy!" he shouts. "I *knew* it was you!"

"Sasha!" Indy exclaims. "I don't believe it!"

Turn to page 53.

Directly beneath the trap door, a stairway leads down to the castle basement and into a long corridor. Torches mounted on the decaying stone walls light the way to a single closed door at the corridor's end. In the dim light you can see an ornate letter D carved on the face of the door.

"This looks like the place," Indy whispers. "Keep your fingers crossed...." Indy opens the door. You gasp. The room is piled high with jewels and gold ingots! You've found Prince Dracula's treasure chamber!

As the three of you stare in awe at your discovery, you hear shouts from above. "Find them!" you hear a voice cry. "Find them or you will all suffer!"

"We haven't got much time!" Indy says. "The Cup of Djemsheed must be in here someplace—let's find it before it's too late!"

You and Indy are searching for the cup when you notice Mihail staring at a crown and cape lying in a corner of the room. As if mesmerized, he slowly puts them on.

"The cup!" Indy suddenly cries out. He's found it! You are about to congratulate him when the door flies open and the Friends of Dracula rush in!

Turn to page 92.

On your way to the airport Mihail tells you that he had managed to trace the Cup of Djemsheed as far as Bucharest, the capital of Romania, before he discovered that he was being followed.

"That's where we're going," Indy says. "By the time Akermann finds out where we are, the cup should be in safe hands—*ours*."

The three of you buy tickets for the next flight to Bucharest, and before long you're boarding the plane. You settle into your seat, exhausted, and fall into a deep sleep.

After what seems like only a few moments, Indy is shaking you awake. "Rise and shine, kid," he says. "We're here." With sleep-filled eyes you look out the airplane window—and see the ancient city of Bucharest!

Turn to page 75.

You're expecting the worst, but nothing happens. You look up and see that the man is clutching his throat. Indy's bullwhip is wrapped tightly around his neck.

"Drop the gun!" Indy shouts, and the man quickly complies. Indy loosens the whip and the man falls, gasping for air.

"Thanks, Indy," you groan. "But the other men...where did they—"

"They're making a run for it," Indy answers.

You look out the restaurant window and see the other three men pile into a car at the curb.

"Maybe we should follow them!" you say.

"Maybe," Indy replies thoughtfully. "Or maybe the man they left behind can tell us what we need to know!"

You know Indy has a point. But what if your prisoner refuses to talk? If you can follow the others, they might lead you to something important to Mihail's search!

If you think you should follow the three men, turn to page 78.

If you decide to interrogate your prisoner, turn to page 26.

"Do not shoot!" Mihail suddenly cries out from beneath the werewolf. "I remember now! I know where we are!"

The werewolf looks down at Mihail, and you think you can see a glimmer of recognition in his deep brown eyes. In an instant the werewolf leaps to his feet and begins to talk to Mihail in Romanian.

Mihail smiles and embraces the werewolf. Neither you nor Indy can hear what they are saying, or understand why they are acting like two long-lost friends.

Finally Mihail explains. "It's remarkable," he says. "I *knew* this place looked familiar, but it was the sudden appearance of my hirsute young friend that made me remember. He thought we were superstitious peasants seeking to harm him, so he attacked us. But when he saw my face, he recalled that I had visited his home on an archeological expedition many years ago."

"Then you know where we are?" Indy asks.

"Why, certainly," Mihail replies. "We are just outside the village of the Lupan, and my young friend wants us to return with him and meet his family!"

....

If you want to go with the werewolf, turn to page 32.

If you would rather try to find your way down from the mountains, turn to page 62.

Leaving the dead Romanians behind, you, Indy, and Mihail turn your attention to the castle. Most of it has all but collapsed after centuries of neglect, but a single wooden door remains intact. As you approach you see that the door has been left ajar.

"Someone forgot to close it on the way out," you say.

"Or on the way *in*," Indy says, swinging the door open wide. "C'mon, kid. Let's take a look."

Inside, the castle is a shambles. There are cobwebs everywhere, and piles of rubble cover the floor. You stumble from room to room through the semidarkness, and when you get to the basement, you hear the sound of laughter coming from behind an ornately carved door.

"Stay here, kid," Indy says, preparing to kick the door open. "I'm going to pay our host a surprise visit."

· ·

Turn to page 68.

You begin to walk across the moat. The ground below the water seems sticky, and as you get closer to the castle you realize that you are sinking. It's quicksand!

You try to escape, but you only sink deeper and faster. In seconds the water is up to your neck. Desperately you cry for help.

"Hang on, kid!" you hear Indy shout. But his voice is far away. Will he get to you in time? Or will this be...

THE END

Holding on to your gun just to be safe, you watch as the wolves jump up at the old man. They yelp happily as they lick his face, and he chuckles as he pets their thick brown fur.

"There, there," he says to them. "I shall feed you in a moment. But first I'd like you all to meet my guests." He turns to you, Indy, and Mihail. "You see?" he says. "I told you the wolves were my friends. They wait for me to come home every night."

"That's just fine," Indy says skeptically. "As long as you don't intend to feed them *us*!"

"Certainly not!" the old man replies, offended. "We are all vegetarians here—come inside and I will show you!"

Feeling a bit more at ease, you put your gun back under your belt and follow the old man into his cottage.

. . . .

Turn to page 64.

"Look at her ring," you whisper to Indy as he takes the glass from the stewardess.

Indy winks at you and sniffs his glass of wine. Then he puts the glass back on the stewardess's tray. "I just remembered," he tells her, "I never touch the stuff."

Sensing that something is wrong, Mihail also refuses the wine.

The stewardess's smile fades. "We shall see about that," she hisses, moving toward the pilot's cabin.

Indy turns to you. "Don't panic, kid," he says, curling his bullwhip in his hands, "but I think we're in trouble. Just walk up front, stand next to the cabin door—and be ready to move!"

You get to the door a moment before it opens and a huge man in a fur overcoat strides out. He points a rifle at Mihail. "Very sorry, Mihail Tepes," he says. "But your flight is about to be canceled!"

. . . .

Turn to page 71.

"Sasha, you old Romanian rooster!" Indy says affectionately. "What the heck are you doing robbing trains out here in the middle of nowhere? Last time I saw you was in Prague! Aren't you a tour guide anymore?"

"Well," Sasha explains, "the guide business has not been too good lately. So now I stick up a train every now and then. It is not great work, but it pays the bills!"

Indy smiles. "Where are we, anyway?" he asks.

"We are approaching the Borgo Pass, a narrow trail that cuts through the Transylvanian Alps," Sasha answers. "It is beautiful countryside, but don't let that fool you—it's dangerous! The whole area is filled with vampire worshippers—the Friends of Dracula. Every time they need a human sacrifice for one of their ceremonies, they come here to kidnap innocent people! They live in a castle on the other side of the mountains."

"You wouldn't happen to know the name of that castle, would you?" asks Indy.

"Why, yes," Sasha says. "The local peasants call it...Castle Dracula."

Turn to page 63.

53

"Wh-where did you get that?" Indy asks, stunned.

"I found it at Castle Dracula a long, long time ago," the old man answers. "Why? You like it? If you do, it's yours. To tell you the truth, after three hundred years I'm pretty tired of having it around. It's an ugly-looking thing, don't you think?"

"Sure," Indy replies. "Whatever you say. And if you don't really mind—we'll take it!"

Before long you are ready to go. You thank the old man for his generosity and leave his humble cottage. As he waves good-bye to you,

you are not quite sure if he is crazy or not. But
you are certain that the Cup of Djemsheed is
one of the most valuable gifts you've ever received!

THE END

"We're trapped between those two boulders!" Indy shouts. "We've got to try and shoot our way out—it's our only chance!" Indy starts to fire at the kidnappers, but they're well protected behind the huge boulder on the mountainside.

"You fools!" one of them shouts down at you. "There is no way out—can't you see that you are trapped?"

Indy answers with his gun.

"Very well," the voice says. "We warned you." You stare with growing horror as the kidnappers begin to push at the rock in front of them. The huge boulder moves an inch, then a foot, then a yard, until finally it comes barreling down the hill, heading straight for the space between the other two boulders—the spot occupied by *you!*

THE END

You and Mihail are flung backward as the plane plummets, but Indy manages to grope his way into the pilot's cabin. When the plane levels out, you get back on your feet and rush to Indy's side. To your amazement, he is alone!

"Our crew flew the coop, kid!" he says, pointing out the window at three tiny parachutes floating down toward the Transylvanian Alps. "I'll try to keep us in the air. You and Mihail look for parachutes."

You search the plane and come up with a box of guns, but only one parachute. Thinking that a gun may come in handy later, you slip one under your belt. Then you tell Indy about the single parachute.

"Great," he groans. "Just great. I guess that leaves us with just two choices. Take your pick, kid."

If you think Indy should try to land the plane, turn to page 8.

If you think the three of you should try to hang on to one parachute, turn to page 17.

"Run!" you shout, pushing at Indy to make him move faster.

The three of you race through the tunnel and up the staircase in mere minutes. Exhausted, you stagger toward the mausoleum door and try to push it open. But it won't budge.

"Locked!" you cry desperately. "Who could have done this...?"

Suddenly the stewardess and a group of Romanians appear on the other side of the barred windows in the door. The stewardess smiles pleasantly. "*We* did this," she says. "And now that Mihail Tepes, the last member of the Dracula family, is inside, we can seal the crypt—forever!"

You feel the rats crawling up your legs. Mihail screams in terror. Indy groans and turns pale. The Dracula family mausoleum is going to have at least two extra permanent guests!

THE END

You listen in silence as the safe is emptied and the man leaves the car. Before long, the train begins to move once again. "I hope you know what you're doing, Indy!" you say.

"So do I, kid," Indy answers. "So do I."

Hours later the train once again comes to a stop. But this time you feel your box being lifted into the air and carried up a long staircase. Then, without warning, it is dropped to the ground. You land with a thud.

Crowbars pry at the nails in the coffin and in an instant the lid is removed. The light hurts your eyes for a moment. When you can see, there's a group of black-robed Romanians standing over you. Two of them grab you by your arms and pull you to your feet. Nearby, you notice that Indy and Mihail have received the same treatment.

One of the black-robed Romanians inspects the three of you carefully for a moment. "Welcome to Castle Dracula," he says, smiling triumphantly. Then he speaks to the men who hold you: "Take them to the dungeon!" he orders. "At midnight the Friends of Dracula shall feast— on human blood!"

....
Turn to page 27.

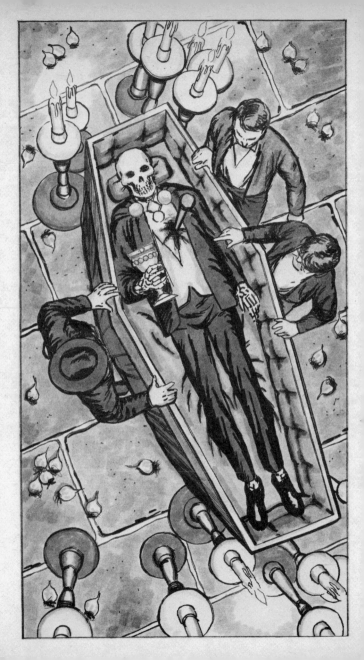

Indy opens the door, and you are awestruck by what you see. Hundreds of candles glow brightly in the room. Cloves of garlic lay scattered about the floor. Huge gold and silver crosses hang from the walls. And in the center of the room rests an open coffin. Mihail and Indy rush over to it and peer inside.

"Thank heaven he is dead," Mihail says, breathing a sigh of relief.

"Thank heaven he's got the cup," Indy says, smiling.

You join them, and see what can only be the skeletal remains of Prince Vlad Dracula. A wooden stake sticks out of his chest, and his bony hand is wrapped tightly around a jewel-encrusted cup—the Cup of Djemsheed!

Turn to page 19.

Indy looks at Mihail in disbelief. "Are you nuts?" he asks. "That guy's a werewolf—just look at him! And you want to meet his family? They'll probably serve dinner—with *us* as the main course! C'mon, kid," Indy adds, grabbing you by the arm. "We're getting out of here."

Mihail and the werewolf remain behind as you and Indy leave the peaceful snow-filled valley. You climb across the mountains for hours, trying to find a way out. Fierce winds whip at you, churning the snow into a blinding blizzard. But above the howling winds you suddenly hear another, more dangerous sound.

Ping! Pee-oow!

A bullet strikes a nearby rock! You and Indy are being shot at! You search for the source of the gunfire. On a mountain ledge, barely visible in the dense snow, are the airplane stewardess and the pilot. "Death to the friends of the vampire!" the stewardess shouts as another bullet narrowly misses you.

"We're sitting ducks, kid!" Indy shouts. "Scatter!"

Turn to page 10.

"Tell me, Indy," says Sasha. "Why are *you* so interested in Castle Dracula? It is all but destroyed. Surely there can be nothing of any value inside it that would interest a famous archeologist like you!"

"You're absolutely right, Sasha," says Indy quickly. "I was just curious, that's all."

There is a sly smile on Sasha's lips, and you realize he's unconvinced.

At that moment you glance out the train window and see the three Romanian kidnappers fleeing into the Borgo Pass. "Indy! They're getting away!" you whisper. "What should we do?"

"I don't know, kid," Indy answers. "Maybe Sasha will take us to the castle—what do you think?"

You know that if you follow the kidnappers they will lead you to Castle Dracula. But they are already far ahead of you. Can you catch up with them before they disappear into the pass? On the other hand, Sasha could lead you to the castle. But he *is* a part-time bandit, and you're not sure you can trust him.

If you chase the kidnappers, turn to page 37.

If you ask Sasha to take you to the castle, turn to page 93.

63

The wolves sit outside the cottage as the old man serves you a delicious meal of soup and home-baked bread. When you finish, he settles back in his chair, lights a cigar, and begins to tell you stories about the history of his country.

"It is amazing," Mihail says after hearing the old man's tale about a war that took place in Romania in the seventeenth century. "I've never heard any of those stories. You must tell me what books you have read on the subject."

"Books?" the old man answers. "I've never read a book in my life! I *saw* those battles take place! I've seen a lot after living for three hundred and fifty years!"

Turn to page 5.

"It's a good thing you waited for us, kid," Indy says. "These moats are always full of traps. We'll make ourselves a bridge and get across that way."

Indy spots a young tree growing on the castle side of the moat. Using his bullwhip, he snares one of its branches and, with great effort, pulls the whip back, bending the young tree over the moat.

"Now crawl across the tree to the other side," Indy grunts, his face turning red. "And hurry—I can't hold this tree down much longer."

As soon as you and Mihail have safely crossed the moat, you see Indy hop onto the tree. The trunk snaps back to its upright position, flinging Indy over the moat. He lands in a heap right beside you.

"Oww," Indy mumbles, rubbing his back as he gets to his feet. "Now let's get a closer look at this castle."

As you inspect the tower you notice a series of small holes carved into the brick. They run up the length of the tower. "I knew I saw someone climbing up these walls before," you say. "They could have been using these!"

"You may be right, kid," Indy says as he places his foot in one of the holes. "Let's try it ourselves!"

Turn to page 38.

You follow the three Romanians, making sure they don't see you. Then you find your-selves down in the museum basement, and you get the funny feeling that you are about to step into a trap. The Romanians are huddled around three rectangular boxes in the huge basement storage room, speaking to each other in hushed whispers.

You rush toward them, but they spot you and dart into a maze of huge storage crates. You attempt to follow, but when you pass the rectangular boxes you stop. The boxes are coffins!

"Indy, come look at this!" you whisper. Then, as the three of you peer inside, you feel something hard come down on your head. Stunned, you fall—right into the coffin!

One of the Romanians hovers over you, a wooden club in his hand. "Seal the other coffins up," he says to his henchmen. "I'll handle this one." As he closes the coffin lid and begins to nail it shut, you black out.

Turn to page 13.

Indy and Mihail follow you back into the dusty bookstore, where the tall thin man greets you by saying, "You come in search of Dracula." His voice is matter-of-fact, his face impassive.

"H-how did you know that?" you ask.

"I know many things," he replies calmly. "Come inside—I shall tell you some of them."

Then he pours you some wine and offers you a seat at a dusty table loaded with stacks of old books.

"It is said that the prince is buried somewhere within a monastery built on an island in Lake Snagov," he says. "But lurking within the monastery is a group of monks that call themselves the Brotherhood of Dracula. It may be dangerous, but I will show you the way there."

Indy and Mihail agree to take him up on his offer, but you think that something about the man is strange. You join them as they follow the man down a shop-lined street. As the four of you pass a mirror, you blink in disbelief! The tall thin man has no reflection!

If you think you should tell Indy, turn to page 120.

If you think it's just your imagination and say nothing, turn to page 88.

67

Indy smashes the carved wooden door and leaps through, leaving you and Mihail behind. Then you hear him gasp. "You!" he exclaims. "How did you get—" His words are cut off by the sound of loud, raucous laughter.

Concerned for Indy's safety, you and Mihail rush through the door. Once inside, you cannot believe your eyes. You are in Prince Dracula's throne room! A gold coffin rests in one corner. Tapestries line the walls. Jewels spill out of an overloaded treasure chest on the floor. And in the center of the room, seated on Prince Dracula's golden throne, is the bearlike Gypsy leader Indy defeated with his bullwhip!

In one hand the Gypsy holds a revolver pointed at Indy. In the other hand he holds...the Cup of Djemsheed! Wine sloshes over the lip of the cup as the Gypsy chuckles drunkenly.

"I hear you tell other Gypsies about your search," he says. "But I get here first. I kill people to make sure you find me." The Gypsy snickers as he leans back on the throne. "You want cup?" he asks Indy. "Well, I want rematch!" He clicks back the hammer of his gun. "And this time," he shouts, "I not lose!"

There is no way that you can stop him from bringing this adventure to...

THE END

As soon as you pull the stake from the coffin, a dense mist fills the room. You can see nothing, but you can hear the members of the Anti-Vampire League shriek fearfully:

"He is unleashed again!"

"He is among us!"

"Run! Run! We must escape!"

You hear the sound of footsteps fleeing the castle, and when the smoke clears, you, Indy, and Mihail are alone once again.

"What did I do?" you ask, bewildered.

"If you remove the stake from a vampire's bones," Mihail says, "it will return to life!" You look inside the coffin. The Cup of Djemsheed is there. But the skeleton is gone!

"It is funny," Mihail muses. "In a way, my hated ancestor saved all our lives." He smiles. "Perhaps Dracula was not such a bad man after all."

"You did good, kid," Indy says, snatching the cup from the coffin. But as you turn to leave the castle, you can only wonder—have you really unleashed the evil Vlad Dracula to roam the earth once again?

THE END

"This is a proclamation ordering the construction of a monastery on an island in Lake Snagov," Mihail says, "signed by my ancestor, Prince Vlad Dracula! I've heard about that monastery. It's been deserted for years, and many people say it's haunted!"

"All the more reason for us to go there right away!" Indy says, a gleam in his eye. "Anything else in that file?"

"Well," Mihail answers, lifting out another scrap of paper. "This map might help us—"

"Hold it right there!" a voice interrupts. You spin around to see Akermann's three thugs standing in the doorway, their guns trained on you. As one of the thugs locks Radu inside the vault, Mihail slips a piece of paper into your pocket. Seconds later the thugs rush you out of the library and into a waiting car. Soon you are in a tiny motorboat on Lake Snagov. In the moonlight you can see the abandoned monastery on a distant island.

"Don't try nothin' funny," one thug warns you. "The boss has plans for you!"

All it would take is a simple push to dump the thugs into the lake. Then you could sneak onto the island unnoticed. But Akermann may already have the cup. It might be better to meet him face-to-face before you make your move.

....

If you push the thugs off the boat, turn to page 95.

If you allow the thugs to take you to Akermann, turn to page 110.

"Now, kid!" Indy shouts.

You spring into action, diving at the man's legs just as his gun goes off. The bullet misses its target, but smashes through one of the windows, instantly depressurizing the plane. The cabin shakes as the air inside rushes out, pulling the startled gunman through the window.

Howling winds scream through the cabin and you feel yourself being tugged toward the open window. Above the din, you can hear Indy's warning:

"Grab something solid, kid!" he shouts. "The pressure will return to normal as soon as the plane slows down!" You grab a seat and hang on for dear life. Then the plane suddenly goes into a nosedive!

Turn to page 57.

The three of you take turns rowing across the lake. It's slow work, and the sun has already set by the time you land on the shore of the island. You see lights glowing brightly inside the monastery, but the beach is strangely silent.

"Something's not right," Indy says as the three of you approach the massive stone building. "You'd think the Brotherhood would have someone standing guard to watch for unwanted visitors. But there's no one here—"

Indy trips over something and staggers. "What was that?" he exclaims. Then you see it. A monk's body, lying at Indy's feet. Next to the body a tunnel has been carved into the monastery's stone walls.

"He must have been guarding *this*!" you exclaim. "I wonder where it leads."

"I think I know," says Indy. "Come on, kid, we've got an appointment to keep!"

Turn to page 89.

Feeling more than a bit chilly from your journey down the snowy mountain, you accept the Gypsies' offer. In moments you are huddled around the campfire, swapping stories with your newfound friends.

As the evening wears on, you notice a young Gypsy girl smiling at Indy. Indy has noticed her too. He smiles back, and tosses in a wink for good measure.

Unfortunately you and the girl aren't the only ones who have noticed Indy. Suddenly a huge, bearlike Gypsy man lunges toward him.

"You like Maria?" he growls as he wraps his pawlike hands around Indy's collar and lifts him off the ground. "Well, she is *mine*—and I crush all men who look at her! Do you want to duel?"

"Do I have a choice?" Indy asks with a gulp.

. . . .

Turn to page 6.

Suddenly Indy puts the handle of his bull-whip in your hands. "Hold on to this as if your life depended on it, kid," he says, "'cause *mine* does!"

Indy drops the other end of the whip out of the mouth of the tunnel and climbs down into the burial chamber. As the chamber walls buckle and heave, Indy races to Akermann's side and slings the frail old man over his shoulder. You hold on to the whip with all your strength as Indy climbs back up and into the tunnel.

You, Indy, Mihail, and Akermann scramble up the tunnel to safety moments before it collapses. The four of you watch in awe as the entire monastery tumbles to the ground.

"Booby-trapped," Indy murmurs. "Prince Dracula wanted to make certain no one ever stole his cup."

"He failed," Akermann says solemnly as he removes the cup from his pocket. "I have it. But you have saved my life, Indiana Jones. For that, the Cup of Djemsheed is yours!"

THE END

"The city of Bucharest has remained unchanged for more than five hundred years," Mihail says as you walk down the narrow cobblestone streets of the ancient city. You pass through a huge open-air market where handmade pottery, colorful embroidered caps, live chickens, and fruit and vegetables are all sold from wooden wagons.

Mihail leads you past the market through a maze of winding streets. "We are heading for the Romanian National Library," he tells you. "It is the largest library in this country, and many ancient historical volumes and maps are stored there, including information that will be vital to our search."

As you walk down the narrow street, you notice a tall, gaunt man standing in the doorway of an old bookstore. To your surprise, he smiles and beckons to you.

....
If you ignore him and keep on going, turn to page 42.

If you want to follow him into his bookstore, turn to page 67.

"I believe I have been here before," says Mihail. "This place seems quite familiar. If only I could remember when I—"

Mihail's words are cut short as a small wiry man suddenly leaps onto his back. The little man pounds at Mihail, forcing him to the ground. Then the two of them thrash about in the snow, locked in a fierce struggle.

You pull the gun from your belt and aim it at the small man. As you cock the trigger, he looks up at you fearfully. His big brown eyes shine in the moonlight, and you can see that his face is completely covered with clumps of matted brown fur. You cannot believe your eyes. He is a werewolf!

....

If you decide to shoot at the creature, turn to page 109.

If you decide to wait and see what happens next, turn to page 48.

You, Indy, and Mihail race out of the restaurant just as the car carrying the Romanians takes off. Indy hails a cab, and the three of you hop inside.

"Follow that car!" cries Indy, and the cab takes off in a burst of speed, flinging the three of you back into your seats. Indy turns to Mihail. "What are we getting ourselves into?" he asks.

"Well, it is like this," Mihail begins. "A group of Romanians has found out about my quest to destroy my ancient ancestor. They call themselves the Friends of Dracula, and they are a fanatical cult of vampire worshippers. They will stop at nothing to keep me from harming Vlad Dracula. Moreover, I believe they plan to sacrifice me to Dracula in some bizarre ritual. Does that answer your question?"

Moments later, when your cab pulls up to the National Museum, you catch a glimpse of the three Romanians as they run inside.

"What do they want in there?" you wonder aloud.

"Only one way to find out, kid," Indy replies, opening the cab door. "Let's go."

Turn to page 66.

Akermann's thugs back away in fear. "I knew this Dracula stuff wasn't on the up-and-up!" one of them says. "Let's get outta here!"

They flee, leaving you, Indy, and Mihail alone with the body of Arbor Akermann. You reach over and take the cup from his hand. There is an inscription carved onto its base:

A LIFE MUST BE TAKEN FOR ETERNAL LIFE TO BE WON.

A strange thrill suddenly courses through your body. Is it only the excitement, or have you just been given the greatest gift of all—eternal life?

As you leave the monastery with the cup, you ask Indy about the inscription. "Well, kid, it *might* be true," he says, smiling, "but you'll have to wait a *looong* time to find out!"

THE END

"Wait!" you cry out fearfully. "We're not evil! We just came here looking for Dracula, and we—"

Your words die on your lips as you see the Gypsy leader's face redden with anger. "Dracula?" he sputters furiously. *"Dracula?!* Spawn of Satan! You three must be destroyed immediately!" The leader motions to the other Gypsies, who push Indy to his knees and hold him still.

"Thanks, kid," Indy mumbles as the Gypsy leader raises his dagger. But just as the dagger is about to strike, Mihail begins to scream at the Gypsy in an unfamiliar Romanian dialect. The Gypsies look at him in horror, make the sign of the cross, and flee as if the devil himself were chasing them.

The three of you run down the hill, leap atop the Gypsies' horses, and race away. Many miles later Indy asks Mihail what he said to the Gypsies to scare them off.

"I told them that I was the son of Dracula," Mihail replies. "And that my father would track them down and destroy them if they hurt me or my friends!"

Turn to page 25.

Indy turns to Mihail. "Do you have any idea what this is all about?"

"Well," Mihail replies sheepishly, "as a matter of fact, I do. This man and his friends are members of the Romanian Anti-Vampire League. They believe that I, like my ancestor Vlad Dracula, am a vampire. They have already followed me across the globe, and they will not rest until I am dead. So you see, Indiana, I must return to Romania for *two* reasons—to search out and destroy my immortal ancestor, and to clear my family name. My life depends on it, and I need your help desperately! If I can locate Dracula's tomb, I am sure that the Cup of Djemsheed will be nearby. Help me, Indiana, and the cup is yours."

Indy says nothing. You know he's thinking that the cup would make a fine addition to the National Museum's collection. Then he smiles. "Okay, Mihail—I'm not sure about this vampire business, but I'd sure like to get a look at the Cup of Djemsheed. Where do we go from here?"

"To Romania," Mihail replies. "Land of the Draculas."

. . . .

Turn to page 94.

Akermann's thugs force you into the monastery. They push you down winding halls to a large stone chamber, where they chain you to the walls. The chamber is empty, except for a closed stone coffin in the center. Atop the coffin lid, shining like a beacon in the dim light, is a golden goblet—The Cup of Djemsheed!

Akermann hobbles into the room, smiling triumphantly. "As you can see," he says, "I have not yet touched the cup. I have been awaiting your arrival, so that you may witness my moment of glory. And now that you are here..."

As Akermann walks slowly toward the cup, you notice a groove in the floor around the coffin. Could it be a trapdoor? Will it open if anyone disturbs the cup?

If you decide to warn Arbor Akermann, turn to page 105.

If you'd rather see what happens when he takes the cup, turn to page 122.

Just then an old werewolf steps up to you. He speaks to Mihail for a few moments and then smiles and shakes his hand. "The village elder remembers me," says Mihail. "We're safe. Now come along—he has invited us to dine with him."

You follow the elder and the other villagers back to the largest of the cottages. Inside, you're seated at the head of a huge table with Indy and Mihail, and served a wonderful Romanian pork stew called *tocana*. After you've eaten, your host offers you a guide to help you get out of the mountains. He warns you, however, that if you are seen in the company of his people by any superstitious peasants, there may be trouble.

If you accept the offer, turn to page 14.

If you think you can find your way out of the mountains without assistance, turn to page 104.

As your eyes adjust to the light, you see hundreds of dimly glowing eyes staring at you. The walls of the tower are lined with huge vampire bats! They flutter about nervously, uncertain of what to make of you. Past them, in a corner of the room, you notice a doorway.

"Through there," Indy whispers, pointing to it. "And walk *quietly*. Remember, we're uninvited guests."

Walking on tiptoe in the darkness, the three of you enter the doorway and stumble down a worn stone stairway that leads deep into the castle.

"Smell that?" Indy says when you are about halfway down. "That's the scent of wet earth. We're probably underground by now."

But as you continue down the stairs, your nose picks up a new odor—garlic! The smell becomes overpowering as you reach the bottom of the staircase and come to a massive wooden door. A light shines out from under it.

"Keep cool, kid," Indy says as he grips the door handle tightly. "We're going in."

....

Turn to page 61.

The mercenaries bind your hands and lead you up the steep mountainside. From the top, you see the remains of an ancient stone castle in the distance.

"Castle Dracula," one mercenary says. "The Friends of Dracula are inside. They will be *very* glad to see you."

Moments later you are at the huge wooden doors of the castle. The mercenary knocks. After a few moments the door opens, and a man wearing a black hood pokes his head out. "Yes?" he says impatiently. "What do you want? We're very busy, you know, and—"

The black-hooded man falls silent when he sees Mihail. Then he smiles. "Oh," he says in a completely different tone of voice. "Please, *do* come in."

He ushers you into a huge room, where twenty robed men kneel at a golden altar. Above the altar is an ancient portrait of a dark man wearing a black cape and a jeweled crown. "Prince Vlad Dracula!" Mihail exclaims.

Turn to page 119.

The thugs drive far out into the country-side. They finally turn into a long driveway and then pull up at the entrance to a huge mansion.

They drag the three of you out of the car and into the mansion, where a thin, stooped old man holding himself up with a cane awaits you in an oak-paneled study.

"I am Arbor Akermann," he croaks, "and as you can see, I'm not as young as I used to be. I have spent many years searching for the secret of eternal youth—with little success." He points his cane at Mihail. "*You* were close to finding the Cup of Djemsheed. My men followed your every move. Then you gave up the search to ask Mr. Jones for help.

"I *need* the cup," Akermann continues hoarsely. "Without its rejuvenating effects, I cannot live much longer. Help me find it! I must have it!"

"Sorry, Akermann," Indy says, "but you'll just have to live and die like the rest of us! When *we* find the cup, it's going straight to the National Museum!"

"Very well," Akermann replies. "If you choose not to help me in my search, then I must make sure you will not *hinder* me—or any-one—ever again. Guards!" he shouts. Three thugs appear at the door. "Take them away."

Turn to page 118.

"You three are not the first people who have come to me today seeking knowledge of Dracula and his monastery," the thin man says as you walk toward Lake Snagov. "There was another. One named Akermann."

"What did you tell him?" Indy asks urgently.

"Only the location of the monastery," answers the man. "Perhaps we shall meet him there."

You groan in dismay at his words. Getting to the Cup is going to be tougher now, but you decide you'd better make the trip anyway. Soon you are on a small motorboat skipping over the waters of Lake Snagov. In the distance you can see the ancient monastery looming up in the late afternoon sun.

The island appears to be deserted. No other boats rest on the shoreline. The thin man leads you to the monastery doors. He swings them open...

...and a group of red-robed monks dive out at you, spears in their hands!

Turn to page 107.

As you crawl through the tunnel you can hear voices chanting far away. Following the sounds, the three of you come to a fork in the tunnel. One tunnel leads down deeper into the ground; the other continues straight ahead.

"Go straight," Indy says. "That's where the sounds are coming from!"

The chanting grows louder as you rush toward a dim light at the end of the tunnel, but an iron grille blocks the way out. Peering through, you see a huge room below you. A hundred robed monks are bowing reverently before a painting of Vlad Dracula as they chant his name over and over again. The Brotherhood of Dracula! Suddenly the chanting stops as the sound of an alarm bell fills the room.

"Intruders in the burial chamber!" one of the monks screams. "Stop them!" You see the monk's face. It's the tall thin man from the bookstore!

"Burial chamber?" you ask Indy. "What are they talking about?"

"I think I know, kid," Indy answers. "Come on. We've got some traveling to do!"

Turn to page 98.

You, Indy, and Mihail bolt toward the huge rock. Bullets whiz past your head as you scurry to safety. Together the three of you leap over a small ledge—and land right in the nest of a gigantic, hungry vulture!

The vulture picks and claws at you, but you must fight it. To attempt to flee would be suicide.

"Stay away from its beak!" Indy shouts as the bullets fly overhead. "Just try to grab it by the neck and hang on!"

Long moments pass as the three of you battle the flying scavenger. You have just about knocked the fight out of it when you notice that the shooting has stopped.

"Hmmm," Indy mutters. "Doesn't sound right to me!"

You peek over the rock and see that the Romanians are lying motionless on the ground near the castle. Cautiously the three of you climb up the hill to get a closer look.

Indy inspects the bodies. "Someone *killed* these guys," he murmurs.

"Someone," Mihail says with a shudder, "or some*thing*!"

Turn to page 49.

When the Friends of Dracula see Mihail, they stop dead in their tracks. Then they kneel. "Praise be to Dracula," they chant. "He has returned to walk among us!"

Indy stares at his Romanian friend. "Y'know, Mihail," he says, "when you're wearing that cape and crown I gotta admit—there *is* a family resemblance!"

You and Indy head for the door, but Mihail makes no move to join you.

"Come on, Mihail," Indy says. "We've got the cup—let's go!"

Mihail smiles vacantly. "You go," he says, "and take the cup with you. I think I shall stay here and get to know these people a little better!"

You and Indy leave the castle knowing that the last of the Draculas has found a new home!

THE END

"About that castle," you say to Sasha as the kidnappers disappear behind a distant mountain. "Could you take us there?"

"Why, certainly," Sasha says smoothly. "Follow me. My men are just outside." As you step off the dark train and into the sunlight, you see Sasha's fellow bandits, a seedy-looking group of about twenty men. They are dressed in colorful tatters, and their unshaven faces bear the scars of many battles.

"Wait here," Sasha tells you. "I must talk to my men before we leave. Some of them are superstitious, but I will convince them that there is no danger in going to the castle."

Sasha walks over to the men and they huddle around him. You cannot hear what he is saying, but when he is finished the bandits look at you and smile greedily.

"I got a feeling Sasha's guessed our little secret, and promised his men a piece of the action," Indy whispers. "I don't like the looks of this, kid, but I guess we haven't got any choice. Let's go!"

Turn to page 40.

After stopping to pick up your passports, you, Indy, and Mihail race to the airport and board the first flight to Romania. As you settle into your seats, you notice that you are the only passengers on the plane.

When you are high over the Transylvanian Alps, a stewardess dressed in a flowing black gown comes down the empty aisle toward you. In her pale white hands she carries a tray with three glasses of deep red wine.

"Compliments of Romaniair, sirs," she says, her bright red lips curling in a smile. "Please drink deeply."

But as she hands Indy a glass you notice the ring on her finger. Is that a coffin on its face?

If you say nothing and allow Indy to drink the wine, turn to page 36.

If you tell Indy about the ring, turn to page 52.

You, Indy, and Mihail exchange glances as the thugs stand in a circle around you. Wordlessly you count the number five on your hand for Indy and Mihail to see. They wink and nod. Then the three of you begin a silent countdown.

Five...four...three...two...*one!*

Together the three of you leap up and at the thugs. Taken by surprise, they fall, screaming, into the cold waters of Lake Snagov.

Indy scrambles to the outboard engine and finds the accelerator. The boat roars off in the direction of the monastery, leaving the thugs far behind.

Within moments you're on shore and walking toward the monastery. The island is eerily silent.

"Akermann's already in there," Indy says. "The only question is, has he found the cup? We've got to get into the monastery—if we can find the entrance. Let's split up. First one to find a way inside, just give a shout and we'll come running."

The three of you head off in opposite directions. You are wandering through some dense bushes when you hear a familiar voice cry out in the darkness. It's Mihail! Racing toward the sound of his cries, you meet up with Indy just in time to see the monastery's massive wooden doors slam shut.

Turn to page 113.

As you stare in awe at the portrait, a fierce hot wind suddenly whips at your backs, blowing you through the castle doors. The instant you are outside, the doors slam shut.

You step back to get a better look at the ancient castle, and see a huge ball of flame burst from the top of the tower. With a deafening roar, the entire castle collapses upon itself. Seconds later, smoldering rubble is all that is left of Castle Dracula.

"Whew!" Indy says. "When those Friends of Dracula decide to have a party, they don't kid around! Looks like this time they *really* brought the house down!"

"But what about the cup?" you ask Indy.

"It probably never existed," Indy answers. "And if it *was* in the castle, we'll never find it now. C'mon, kid. Let's go home."

As you, Indy, and Mihail leave the remains of Castle Dracula behind, you think about the stranger who freed you. You shudder. You can never be certain that he was Dracula, but your memory of him will stay with you for the rest of your life!

THE END

The three of you scramble back through the tunnel until you return to the fork you saw earlier.

"This is some kind of ventilation system," Indy explains. "If we go *this* way," he says, pointing to the tunnel that leads downward, "we should end up in one of the lower levels—possibly the burial chamber those monks were so worried about!"

You follow Indy and soon come to the end of the tunnel. Indy guessed right! Below you is an ancient burial chamber. Next to a stone coffin stands Arbor Akermann and his thugs, preparing to remove the coffin lid.

Unseen, you watch as the doors burst open and the monks rush in. "Don't touch that coffin!" one of them screams. But it is too late. The lid slides off, exposing the skeleton of Prince Dracula. The Cup of Djemsheed is in his hand.

The walls begin to quake as Akermann clutches at the golden goblet. Chunks of stone fall from the ceiling. The monks and Akermann's men flee from the burial chamber in mortal terror, leaving Akermann behind. You know the old man will never be able to make it to safety without assistance. He is helpless.

....

If you decide to try to save Akermann, turn to page 74.

If you'd rather just try to save yourselves, turn to page 100.

98

The bandits rush in and begin to load their sacks with jewels and precious objects. Overcome with greed, they don't even notice Indy as he walks over to the cup. Stealthily, he grabs it and slips it under his jacket.

"I got it," he whispers to you. "Now let's get out of h—"

"A moment, please," Sasha interrupts, grabbing Indy by his arm. The cup slips out from under Indy's jacket and clangs to the floor. "What have we here?" Sasha says as he picks up the priceless object. "I do believe there is a *thief* in our midst."

The other bandits stop their looting and glare at you angrily. You gulp, uncertain of what will happen next.

"It is but a trinket!" Sasha laughs, breaking the tense silence. "If that is all you want, Indiana Jones, you may take it! Now go!"

You don't need to be told twice. The three of you race from the castle and head back to civilization, knowing that you have escaped with the greatest treasure of all.

THE END

"Let's get out of here!" you shout to Indy as huge chunks of stone fall from the ceiling of the chamber. "Prince Dracula must have booby-trapped his coffin to keep anyone from stealing the cup! The whole monastery's caving in!"

Frantically, you scurry back up the tunnel, leaving Akermann, his men, and the monks far behind. You have almost made it to safety when the tunnel walls begin to vibrate. The three of you leap out of the tunnel just as it collapses.

Standing on the shore, you watch as the monastery crashes to the ground. As you head back to Bucharest you know that both the cup and the Brotherhood of Dracula are gone forever, and that your adventure has come to...

THE END

You crawl down the dark winding tunnel, sweeping aside ancient spider webs that stick to your hands and face. Soon the tunnel opens out on a small empty room. On its far side, a stairway leads up into the monastery above. In the center of the room is a large stone coffin covered with a thick layer of dust.

"I think this is it, kid!" Indy exclaims. He wipes the dust off the coffin to reveal an ornate letter—the letter D, carved on its lid. The tomb of Dracula! You can hardly contain your excitement as you push the heavy coffin lid open.

A cloud of centuries-old dust rises up out of the coffin and blinds you for a moment. When it clears, you see the skeleton of Vlad Dracula, with the Cup of Djemsheed clutched tightly in its bony hand!

Indy reaches for the cup. At that moment Arbor Akermann hobbles down the stairs and into the room. "Give me the cup," he demands. "Give it to me now!"

"Not on your life!" Indy answers defiantly.

"No, not on *my* life," Akermann says, pointing to the doorway as Mihail steps into view. "But perhaps on *his* life." One of Akermann's thugs is holding a gun to Mihail's head.

Turn to page 116.

Indy thanks the Lupan elder for his offer, but decides to head down the mountains alone. The elder points you in the right direction, and after thanking him for his hospitality, the three of you leave the village and start your journey.

A few hours later you are at the base of the mountains, with a lush green field stretching before you. A band of Gypsies has set up camp there, and are sitting around a huge fire. As the three of you approach, they look up at you and smile.

"Do not be afraid, fellow wanderers," one of them says, waving for you to come closer. "The night air is cold: you are welcome to warm yourselves by our fire."

Turn to page 73.

"Wait!" you blurt out. "Don't touch the cup! It's a trap!"

"Come, come," Akermann replies. "Don't you think it's a little late for jokes?"

"I'm serious," you say. "Just look at your feet! You're standing on a trap door!"

Akermann looks at you and laughs. Then he snatches the cup off the coffin lid. As soon as it is in his hand, however, the floor beneath him begins to quake. The stone coffin rocks back and forth, but Akermann, frozen with fear, clutches the stone lid.

A second later the coffin drops through the ground, taking both Akermann and the Cup of Djemsheed with it. Long moments pass as the three of you and Akermann's men listen for a sound, but hear nothing.

"Bottomless," you murmur solemnly. Then you hear a soft thud.

"Almost bottomless," Indy says.

Without a leader, Akermann's men untie you and leave the monastery. Alone, you, Indy, and Mihail gaze into the pit.

"Well," you say, turning to leave, "looks like the Cup of Djemsheed is gone forever!"

"No way, kid!" Indy says, smiling. "Get me a *looong* rope—I'm going down there!"

As you return Indy's smile, you know that before long the Cup of Djemsheed will be yours!

THE END

As the two men argue, the other mercenaries and the Friends of Dracula gather around, leaving you, Indy, and Mihail unguarded. Indy walks behind you and drops to his knees. With his teeth, he loosens the ropes around your hands and in seconds you are free. As you untie Indy and Mihail, Indy points to a trap door near the golden altar. "This is our chance to find the cup," he whispers. "And I'm betting we'll find it under there. Let's go!"

The three of you creep toward the altar. Then the mercenaries draw their guns on the Friends of Dracula.

"No more arguing," one mercenary says. "The deal's off. We'll find someone else to buy them—you're not the only group of vampire worshippers in the world, y'know!"

"You are not taking them anywhere!" the treasurer bellows angrily. He gestures to the other Friends of Dracula and they swarm over the stunned mercenaries like a pack of rats. The mercenaries scream in pain and fear as they disappear under a sea of black hoods.

"I hope you know what you're doing," you gulp as Indy opens the trap door and motions for you to enter.

"So do I, kid," Indy answers. "So do I."

....
Turn to page 44.

"To the tombs!" the thin man says, grinning evilly. Obediently, the monks hustle you inside and lead you down to the monastery cellar. There you see an enormous stone coffin with the letter D engraved on the lid. Chained to the walls around the coffin are hundreds of skeletons. Among them are Arbor Akermann and his three thugs! The monks grab you, Indy, and Mihail, and soon you too are hanging from the wall.

"We are the Brotherhood of Dracula," the tall, thin man says, "and it is our mission to see to it that neither the tomb of Dracula nor the Cup of Djemsheed inside it is ever disturbed by human hands. The skeletons you see around you were fools like you who came in search of the cup. Get to know them. You shall soon share their fate."

THE END

"Do your worst," the tall thin man says, a defiant look in his eye. "I will tell you nothing!"

"I have heard of the Brotherhood of Dracula," Mihail says grimly. "They are said to follow the old ways of my ancestor. We must be very careful when we get to the monastery, Indy. Now come," he adds, tugging Indy away from the tall man. "The lake is not far from here."

Indy grudgingly agrees, and soon you are standing at the shore of Lake Snagov. Indy asks a local fisherman about renting a boat, and the man leads you to a broken-down rowboat. "Here she is," he says proudly. "Isn't she a beauty?" As the three of you climb aboard, the fisherman asks, "Are you having a party out there?"

"What do you mean?" asks Mihail.

"Well," answers the man, "this is the second boat I rented to Americans today!"

Indy gulps. "Uh-oh! I think I know who those other Americans are!"

....
Turn to page 72.

"Kid, don't!" Indy shouts.

But it is too late. With a deafening roar, you fire the gun, missing the werewolf by miles. As the creature scampers off, the sound of the gun echoes across the mountains, only to be replaced by a rumbling sound that grows louder with each passing second.

"Now you've *really* done it, kid," Indy groans.

You look up and see waves of snow cascading off the mountaintops toward you. You've started an avalanche—and finished your adventure!

THE END

Akermann's thugs deliver the three of you to the island. In front of the monastery's huge wooden doors, a group of men awaits you, led by Akermann himself. He hobbles forward to greet you. "Wonderful evening, isn't it?" he asks.

"It *was*," Indy answers. "Until we met you and your friends."

"Don't be bitter, Jones," Akermann replies. "You three did a wonderful job of leading me here. All I had to do was phone the airline and ask where you were bound. When they told me you were going to Bucharest, I knew that my precious cup was not too far off. I had my men break into the library archives so I could take a look at the Dracula file, and I learned all about this monastery—not to mention its wonderful contents. And now the cup is mine." Then, addressing his men, Akermann adds, "Take them inside. We are ready to begin."

Turn to page 83.

You strike the match and the room seems to explode with light. Then you see them—thousands of huge vampire bats lining the walls and ceiling! The flame disturbs their sensitive eyes, and they begin to flap their wings and screech angrily.

"Uh-oh," says Indy.

You drop the match to the floor seconds before the bats swarm over you. As they scratch and bite your body you flail this way and that, trying to get away, but when you hear Indy and Mihail's tortured screams you know it's hopeless. The force of the attacking bats pushes you out the window and sends you plummeting—to the quicksand moat below.

THE END

You rush up to the monastery doors and try to pull them open, but they are locked.

"Well," Indy says, "there's got to be another way inside!"

"There better be!" you say. "It's getting cold out here!" You shove your hands deep into your pockets and feel an unfamiliar piece of paper. Then you remember what it is.

"Indy," you exclaim, pulling the yellowed paper out of your pocket. "Mihail took this from the library and slipped it to me just as Akermann's goons grabbed us!"

Indy examines the paper, which begins to crumble at his touch. "This is fantastic!" he says. "It's a map of the entire monastery—including secret passages that will lead us right to the cup! Come on, kid! We've still got a chance!"

With the map's help, Indy finds a small hollow dug into the side of a hill. You have to crouch to get inside. As soon as you do, an iron gate slams shut behind you, blocking your exit.

"Looks like a one-way street," Indy murmurs. "Let's go."

Turn to page 101.

The bandits are busy shooting at a group of black-robed figures who are darting around the room in fear and confusion. "They are the Friends of Dracula," Mihail says. "Sasha and his men must have surprised them in the middle of one of their rituals!" As the attack continues, the Dracula worshippers flee through a tiny hole in the castle wall.

When the fighting is over, you join Sasha inside. His men scurry about the castle, exploring every nook and cranny in the hopes of finding something worth stealing.

"Looking for something, Sasha?" Indy asks.

"We shall know in a minute," Sasha replies.

At that moment a bandit standing on the far side of the castle points to a doorway and

shouts happily. "I found it!" he cries. "Come and see! Come and see!"

Sasha races into the room, with you, Indy, and Mihail close behind. Bags of priceless gems are piled along its walls, and gold ingots are stacked up to the ceiling. A skeleton lies next to a solid-gold table.

"The remains of Vlad Dracula!" Mihail whispers in awe. But you do not hear him. Your eyes are glued to the jewel-encrusted cup resting upon the table. You cannot believe it. You have found it—the Cup of Djemsheed!

Turn to page 99.

"I'm sorry, Indy," Mihail stammers. "I *had* to tell them. They threatened to kill me...."

Indy nods and hands the cup to Akermann.

"Thank you," says the old man. He reaches into his pocket and pulls out a vial filled with a thick, red liquid. Then he pours the liquid into the cup and watches with satisfaction as it bubbles furiously.

"You don't know how long I've waited for this," he says. "In moments I shall be young for all eternity!" He raises the cup into the air. "A toast," he cries, "to *my* health!" Then he drains the cup in a swallow.

A moment passes. Then another. Akermann waits for something to happen, but when it does, he is unprepared. He grabs at his neck, as if he is choking. Then he doubles over and falls to the ground, writhing in pain. You rush to help him, but you are too late. Arbor Akermann is dead.

Turn to page 79.

As Indy and Mihail continue on, you stop to take a peek inside the mausoleum, and see a stairway leading down below the ground. "Hey, Indy! Mihail!" you shout excitedly. "This way! Hurry!"

You climb down the stairs and into a long, narrow tunnel. At the end of the tunnel is a single door.

"What do you think is behind it?" you ask breathlessly.

"I wouldn't know, kid," Indy says with a smile. "But if you'd like to find out..." He points to the door handle.

You grip the handle, open the door...

...and hundreds of skeletons fall out on top of you!

Turn to page 23.

At gunpoint, the guards lead you outside the mansion and lock you inside a long, fenced-in yard. "Akermann must be crazy if he thinks we can't get out of this," Indy says. But when he touches the fence, an electric charge jolts through his body, knocking him to the ground. Then a door at the end of the yard opens, and a pack of snarling mastiff dogs charges at you. You steel yourself for their attack as Indy staggers to his feet.

"We've got one chance, kid," he says groggily, pointing to some tree branches hanging over the fence. With a snap of his whip he snags the thickest branch, climbs up the whip, and swings gracefully over the fence! With seconds to spare, you and Mihail follow.

You find an empty limousine in front of the mansion. Luck is with you—the keys are in the ignition! The three of you hop inside and are soon streaking away from Akermann's mansion.

"Where to now, Indy?" you ask.

"A quick stop to get our passports," Indy replies. "Then, to the airport. We're taking the next flight...to Romania!"

....
Turn to page 46.

As soon as you enter the room, the hooded men come at you, arms outstretched. The three of you are helpless as they push you to the ground and swarm over you greedily.

Suddenly there's a gunshot, and the hooded men leap away from you in fear.

"Back off!" shouts a mercenary, brandishing a smoking gun. "You don't get these guys until *we* get paid!" He looks around the room. "Who's in charge here?" he asks. "It's time we talked turkey!"

One of the hooded men steps forward. "I am the treasurer of the Friends of Dracula," he announces. "We must sacrifice Mihail Tepes in honor of our master. Therefore, I am prepared to pay a thousand lei for him."

"That's all?" The mercenary snorts. "What about the other two? They ought to be worth something!"

The treasurer shakes his head. "They are of no use to us. Only Mihail is a true Dracula— only he can be sacrificed. As for the others— take them back."

"What?" the mercenary answers angrily. "Now wait a minute—"

Turn to page 106.

"Indy," you whisper as you follow the thin man through empty streets, "I think that guy's a vampire—he's got no reflection!"

"Must be your imagination, kid," Indy replies. "Even so, I'm not sure I trust him myself! Let's keep an eye on him."

Soon the man points to an alley. "In there," he says. You walk inside, only to discover a dead end.

"Hey," Indy says angrily. "Is this your idea of a joke?"

The thin man pulls a gun out from under his coat. "This is no joke," he says grimly. "You are too dangerous to the Brotherhood of Dracula to be allowed to live!"

In a blur of speed, Indy pulls out his whip and cracks it at the thin man, snapping the gun out of his hand. The man falls, whimpering in pain.

"Boy," you say to Indy, "I never thought you'd use that old trick again!"

"Why not?" Indy replies. "Works like a charm every time!" He walks over to the man and grabs him by the shirt. "What's the big idea, buddy?" he asks.

Turn to page 108.

"What are you looking at?" Akermann shouts as you silently stare at the groove in the floor. He follows your eyes to the groove and looks at it thoughtfully. Then he smiles and steps away from the coffin. Using his cane, he knocks the cup off the coffin lid. It clangs to the ground and rolls into a corner; the coffin drops through the floor into a deep pit below!

"Thought I would fall in with the coffin, did you?" Akermann smirks. "Well, *you* three are the only ones going in there today! But first," he continues, "we have a little business to discuss. It is a little matter of blood. Blood that must be used to fill the cup in order for it to work its magic. Blood that you three will provide!"

As you trade frightened glances with Indy and Mihail, you realize that you will never know if the legend of the Cup of Djemsheed is true!

THE END